In memory of Crusoe,
a most excellent cat, though no Hero. P.P.

For Lily. I.B.

THIS IS A BORZOI BOOK PUBLISHED BY ALFRED A. KNOPF

Text copyright © 2000 by Philip Pullman
Illustrations copyright © 2000 by Ian Beck
Designed by Ian Butterworth

All rights reserved under International and Pan-American Copyright
Conventions. Published in the United States of America by Alfred A. Knopf,
a division of Random House, Inc., New York, and simultaneously in Canada by
Random House of Canada Limited, Toronto. Distributed by Random House, Inc.,
New York. Originally published in Great Britain by Transworld Publishers,
a division of the Random House Group Ltd, in 2000.

KNOPF, BORZOI BOOKS,
and the colophon are registered trademarks of Random House, Inc.

www.randomhouse.com/kids

Library of Congress Cataloging-in-Publication Data
Pullman, Philip, 1946-
Puss in Boots : the adventures of that most enterprising feline / written by
Philip Pullman ; and illustrated by Ian Beck.-1st ed.
p.   cm.
Summary: A clever cat wins his master a fortune and the hand of a princess.
[1. Fairy tales. 2. Folklore-France.] I. Beck, Ian, ill.   II. Puss in
Boots. English. III. Title.
PZ8.P97 Pu 2001
398.2'0944'04529752-dc21
[E]   00-062931

ISBN 0-375-81354-3 (trade)

Printed in Belgium

August 2001

10 9 8 7 6 5 4 3 2 1

First American Edition

Puss  in Boots

The Adventures of That Most Enterprising Feline

Written by Mr. Philip Pullman
and illustrated by Mr. Ian Beck

Alfred A. Knopf New York

Once upon a time, there was an old miller who died and left all his property to his three sons. The eldest son got the mill, the middle son got the donkey, and as for the youngest son, Jacques, all he got was —

"The cat?" said Jacques. "Father's left me the cat?"

He was a fine cat, but not much use when it came to earning a living.

Little do you know, Master.

The mill itself wasn't much of a gift, either. The mill wheel was stuck and, hard as they tried, the three brothers couldn't make it turn.

And to make things worse, a letter came from their landlord, Monsieur Ogre. He was raising their rent.

Jacques decided that since the mill couldn't support all three of them, he'd have to leave and seek his fortune.

"I've only got ten pence in the world, Puss," he said, scratching his head.

Jacques couldn't believe his ears. But there was no doubt about it — Puss was talking, all right.

"Yes, Master," he said. "Give me the money, and I'll go and buy some boots. I can get them cheap — I killed some rats for the cobbler yesterday. . . ."

Soon, Puss came back dressed like a gentleman of wealth and fashion.

"We've got a great career ahead of us, Master!" said Puss.

"We've got all the qualities we need. At least, I've got the wit, if you'll supply the courage."

So off they went to seek their fortune together.

But it wasn't long before they felt hungry. Courage and wit were all very well, but what they needed then was food. However, as soon as Jacques had bagged a couple of partridges, Puss made off with them.

"I've got a plan, Master," he said. "It's such a good plan I can't explain it. But you'll soon see!"

Meanwhile, someone else was feeling hungry, too. In his foul and filthy castle, the Ogre was getting peckish.

FOOD! Bring me food! Doesn't anyone understand how hungry I am? And where's that rent?

Carrying out his plan, Puss went straight to the Royal Palace. He looked so impressive that all the sentries saluted and all the servants bowed, and soon Puss was in the presence of the King of France himself, together with his beautiful daughter.

"A thousand greetings from my master, the Marquis of Carabas!" he said. "Please accept this poor gift of partridges from his estate."

"How kind," said the King. "I'm partial to partridge."

"Tell us about the Marquis of Carabas," said the Princess. "He must be a generous man."

Aha!

Now's my chance.

"Well, Your Royal Highness," Puss began, "he's a very modest man, and he'd never tell you himself — but he once rescued a whole family from a burning building. The rope caught fire at the top, and he raced the flames to the bottom!"

The King and the Princess were very impressed.

"Not only that," Puss went on, "he fought a whole ship full of Barbary pirates — the very worst sort. Single-handed!"

"My word," said the Princess. "I don't suppose he's married, by any chance?"

"No," said Puss. "The Emperor of China's daughter was in love with him, but he didn't care for her."

I'm so glad.

"Well, Monsieur Puss," said the King, "please take our best wishes to the Marquis of Carabas. You must excuse us now; my daughter and I are just going for a ride along the river."

Good!

Puss quickly thought of a new plan and said, "Your Majesty, the weather's very changeable at this time of year; if you're going near the river, it might be a good idea to take a spare suit of clothes."

"Excellent idea, Monsieur Puss!" said the King.

Puss left at once and hurried ahead to the meadows by the river, where he found some workers mowing the hay.

"Who owns these meadows?" he said.

"Why, the Ogre!" they answered.

"Well, that's all changed. If anyone asks, you're to say that they belong to the Marquis of Carabas, understand?"

As soon as Puss had got that into their heads, he looked for Jacques and found him fishing on the riverbank.

"Feeling hot, Master?" he said. "Why don't you go for a swim?"

"D'you know, I think I will," said Jacques, taking off all his clothes and diving in.

"And then you can pretend to be a Marquis," added Puss, hiding Jacques' clothes.

When the Royal coach went by, Puss waved and cried out.

Help! Help! The Marquis of Carabas is drowning!

Puss explained that they had been attacked by robbers, who had stolen the Marquis' clothes. The King was delighted to help and offered his spare clothes at once. Looking every inch a Marquis, Jacques climbed in the coach with them.

"I wonder who those fine meadows belong to?" said the King.

He stopped the coach to ask, and the mowers, seeing Puss watch them dangerously, said, "The Marquis of Carabas, Your Majesty."

Jacques hardly noticed. He only had eyes for the Princess.

She's ever so beautiful!

He's very handsome...

Meanwhile, the Ogre was feeling unwell. "Send for the Doctor!" he roared. "I'm having conniptions!"

A boiled egg.

Hic!

MOOOOOOo

Goodness me! What did you have for breakfast?

But the Doctor couldn't find anything wrong, so the Ogre sent for the Astrologer.

The Astrologer consulted his charts and announced: "I see great fortune in the stars. As a matter of fact, I see . . . marriage! What you need, Monsieur Ogre, is — a wife."

"Then bring me one at once!" said the Ogre.

His servants brought him pictures of lots of possible wives, and the Ogre looked at them all without finding one that suited him.

But finally he found the one he wanted.

He said to his servant, "This is the lucky girl, no doubt about it. She'll be so pleased when she finds out she's going to marry me! Go and get her right away."

"The Princess, Monsieur Ogre?" said the servant doubtfully. "Well, if you say so . . ."

Back at the Palace, the Princess and Jacques were falling in love, though neither of them quite knew how to say so.

When will he ask me to marry him?

I wish I dared ask her to marry me.

When they were alone, Jacques told Puss how nervous he felt.

"I thought you were going to supply the courage, Master?" said Puss. "Now listen carefully: all you have to do is tell her she's more beautiful than the moon shining through cherry blossoms."

"Moon . . . cherry blossoms," said Jacques. "All right, I'll remember that."

Late that night, the Princess went into the Palace garden because she couldn't sleep. She was so much in love that she didn't hear the Ogre's servants creeping up behind her.

He loves me, he loves me not, he loves me.

The villains bundled her up and carried her away. They left a message addressed to "HIS MADGESTY":

DEAR YOUR MADGESTY,
I AM GOING TO MARY THE PRINCESS AND I THUOUHGT YOU WUOLD LIKE TO KNO. IF YOU TRY TO STOPP ME I WILL EET HER SO THERE.
HOPE YOU ARE KEAPING WELL.

YOURS TRULY, MONSEWER OGRE.

P.S. WHEN WE ARE MARIED WE WILL COME AND STAY WITH YOU AND YOU CAN COME AND STAY WITH US.

"Marry my daughter?" cried the King, outraged. "How dare he? I want his head! I want her back! I want vengeance!"

"Never fear, Your Majesty," said Jacques. "Monsieur Puss and I shall go to Castle Ogre and rescue the Princess!"

"My dear Carabas," said the King, "if you bring her back here safely . . ."

"You'll give him her hand in marriage," Puss prompted.

"Just exactly what I was thinking," said the King. "Off you go, my brave fellows!"

So Jacques and Puss set off, and soon they were deep in a wild forest . . .

And before long, they were completely lost. They wandered for hours until they came to a cave. An old hermit was gathering herbs nearby.

"Father," said Jacques, "we're trying to get to Castle Ogre. Can you tell us the way?"

"You're going to the Ogre?" said the Hermit. "Beware! You'll have to go past the Ghouls. The only way you can do that safely is to give them some of these dream berries — they'll make them drowsy, and you can slip past."

The Hermit told them that the Ogre had once been a great enchanter, but he'd been so greedy that he'd lost most of his magic powers. But he could still do one or two unusual things.

"For example, he can see things that most of us can't," said the Hermit. "If I had the chance, I'd like to ask him why the water in the spring doesn't cure my aching bones as it used to. I'm sure he'd know."

"We'll ask him," said Jacques. "I've got a question of my own to ask him, if it comes to that. Thank you, Father!"

The way led through a ruined graveyard, and they couldn't turn back. But they'd hardly begun to tiptoe through the tombstones when —

"AAARRGGH!" cried Puss, leaping high into the air. "Goo - goo - ghouls!"

"WHAT?" yelled Jacques, terrified. "WHERE? WHERE?"

"Here," said a creaky-croaky voice behind them.

"And here," said a rumbly-mumbly voice ahead of them.

Puss and Jacques stood back to back as the Ghouls crept toward them on ghastly legs.

"We've been awake for a thousand years," said one Ghoul, "and oh, how we long for sleep. . . ."

"If we can't sleep," said the other Ghoul, "we'll take all your bones out through your noses and play pick-up-sticks with 'em, that's what we'll do."

Quickly Jacques threw down some dream berries, and the Ghouls stopped to pick them up.

Dreams! At last!

"Can you tell us how to get to Castle Ogre?" said Jacques.

While one Ghoul explained the way to Jacques, the other beckoned to Puss.

"Since you've been so kind as to bring us the dream berries," he said, "here's a tip for you. The Ogre's got a big trick up his sleeve. . . ." And he whispered the Ogre's secret to Puss.

"So that's it!" cried Puss. "Aha, Monsieur Ogre, we've got you now!"

"Ask him why we can't sleep," said the Ghouls as they waved goodbye.

"We certainly will," said Jacques. "Enjoy your dreams, gentlemen!"

And leaving the Ghouls to their creepy-weepy sleeplessness, Jacques and Puss hurried onward to Castle Ogre.

In a dark and dismal dungeon, the Princess was lamenting her fate. The Ogre intended to marry her the very next day, and she couldn't see any way out.

But suddenly she heard a whisper from the window.
"Don't worry, Your Royal Highness!" said Puss, squeezing through the bars.

"The Marquis of Carabas is on his way!"
"Oh, Monsieur Puss!" she cried. "I'm so glad to see you!"
"We'll get you out, never fear. But before we do, we need your help to ask the Ogre some questions. . . ."
Puss explained, and then he dived beneath the bed, for they heard the Ogre coming.

"My little cuddle pie!" bellowed the Ogre. "Give me a kiss!"

"Oh, Monsieur Ogre, I'll give you all the kisses you want if you can explain the strange dreams I had."

"I can explain any dream," said the Ogre. "Go on! Anything!"

"Well, first I dreamt of an old hermit who lives in the forest. The water in the spring used to cure his aching bones, but it doesn't anymore. Why's that?"

"Easy! A snake has made its nest under the spring. Dig it up, and the water will be as good as ever."

"And then I dreamt that some Ghouls had been awake for a thousand years. Why can't they sleep?"

"Because no one will kiss them good night! Ha ha ha!"

"And finally," she said, remembering what Puss had told her to ask, "I dreamt of a mill where the wheel wouldn't turn. Why is it stuck?"

"The old miller hid something under the wheel. All they have to do is look. That reminds me — they owe me some rent. What about that kiss?"

But before the Princess had to do any kissing, Puss leapt out from under the bed.

"Not so fast, Monsieur Ogre!" he said.

"Who's this?" said the Ogre, amazed.

"One of your greatest admirers," said Puss, bowing low. "I've heard, O mighty and fragrant Ogre, that you are able to change into any animal you want. Can it really be true?"

"Oh, yes," said the Ogre, pleased. "Watch!"

"Marvelous!" said Puss. "What else can you do?"

Truly reptilian splendor, Monsieur!

"I can do a hippo! Look!"

And he did, too. There was hardly room
for them all in the dungeon.

"Astounding!" said Puss. "I wonder . . .
Could you turn into a mouse?"

"Of course! Easy! Watch this −"
In the blink of an eye, the Ogre changed into a mouse. It was the last thing he did.

Got you, you brute!

And while Puss ate the villain up, Jacques was chasing all
the Ogre's men out of the castle for good.

So Jacques and Puss and the Princess set out for home, stopping to carry out some errands on the way.

In the forest, the Hermit was delighted to see them, and soon Jacques had dug out the snake from under the spring.

Finally they went back to the mill. Jacques' brothers were still struggling to get the mill wheel to turn, and they were nearly in despair.

But when they found what their father had hidden beneath it, they could hardly believe their luck.

"And the wheel turns as well as ever," said one brother.

"We can pay the rent at last!" said the other.

"Oh, you won't have to pay rent anymore," said Jacques.

"The Ogre's gone for good."

They all went to the Palace, where the Princess told her father that she was going to marry Jacques. But of course they had to admit that he wasn't really a Marquis at all, and the King was thunderstruck.

"She can't possibly marry a commoner," he said. "It just isn't done. I don't know how we can get round the problem. It's unsolvable!"

"Your Majesty, if I may propose a solution?" said Puss. "All you have to do is make him a Marquis on the spot. Then he can marry the Princess after all."

The King was even more thunderstruck.

"Truly brilliant!" he cried. "I don't know how you think of these things, Monsieur Puss. Did I say Monsieur Puss? I meant Sir Puss, of course!"

So Jacques the miller's son became the Marquis of Carabas in truth as well as in Puss' imagination, and he married the Princess. They went to live in the Ogre's castle and were happy ever after, once they'd cleaned it up.

As for Puss, he went back to doing what he loved most in the world — catching mice, dreaming of glory, and best of all, just snoozing in the sun.